USBORNE EASY READING

The Birthday Su

Felicity Brooks

Models by Jo Litchfield ✿ Designed by Non Figg

Language consultant: Dr. Marlynne Grant Bsc, CertEd, MEdPsych, PhD, AFBPs, CPsychol

Photography by Howard Allman ✿ Edited by Jenny Tyler

This story is about Polly and Jack Dot.

Here they are with Mr. Dot, Mrs. Dot and Pip the dog.

This is Littletown where they all live.

There is a little blue bird to find on every page

Polly, Jack and Mr. Dot go to the baker's.

Mr. Bun, the baker, has baked Polly a birthday cake.
Today is Polly's birthday.

The cake is in a big box.

"Let me see! Let me see!"
says Polly. "Not yet," says Mr. Dot. "It's a surprise."

Mr. Dot carries the cake.

"Have fun," calls Mr. Bun.
"Be careful with the cake!"

BUMP! "Be careful with
the cake!" says Mr. Dot.

CRASH! "Be careful with
the cake!" says Jack.

TRIP! "Be careful with
the cake!" says Polly.

Mr. Dot bumps the postman.
He almost drops the cake.

Mr. Dot slips on the road.
He almost drops the cake.

"The box is a little
squashed," says Jack.

"Were you careful with
the cake?" asks Mrs. Dot.

They take the cake into the kitchen.

Mrs. Dot takes off the ribbon.
Polly peeks inside the box.

It's a clown cake!

The clown has red hair, big shoes and a bow tie.

"What a wonderful cake!" says Polly. "I love clowns!"

Pip likes the look of the clown cake, too.

Pip jumps up and barks. Who's that at the door?

It's a real clown!

The clown has a big bag.
Pip sniffs his big shoes.

Polly is happy. She
shakes the clown's hand.

It's time for Polly's party.

Here are Polly's friends. They give her presents.
But where is the clown?

Up jumps the clown.
BOO!

He pulls a tree
out of his bag.

It grows and
grows and grows.

He stands on one hand, makes balloon animals and juggles.

He is very funny.

He puts his hand in his bag.

He pulls out a pink pie.

Oh dear! Now he trips.

SPLAT!

Everyone laughs, even the clown.

Polly blows out her candles.

It's time to eat. Polly likes her clown cake best.
"I'll give some to the real clown," she says.

But where is the clown?

He isn't under the table.

He isn't under the stairs.

He isn't behind the sofa.

And he isn't in the kitchen.

They can't find him anywhere.

It's time to go home.

Polly's friends say goodbye.
Polly wishes the clown had said goodbye too.

Polly goes outside to wave to her friends.

Out comes Mr. Bun. Polly is surprised to see him.
"I came to see if you were careful with the cake," he says.

Jack looks at Mr. Bun's bag.

"I think Mr. Bun was your birthday surprise," says Jack.
What do *you* think Jack means?